The HOUND of the BASKERVILLES

A Sherlock Holmes Mystery

by Sir Arthur Conan Doyle

retold by Martin Powell

illustrated by Daniel Perez

LIBRARIAN REVIEWER
Katharine Kan
Graphic novel reviewer and Library Consultant

READING CONSULTANT
Elizabeth Stedem

www.raintreepublishers.co.uk
Visit our website to find out
more information about
Raintree books.

To order:
☎ Phone 0845 6044371
🖨 Fax +44 (0) 1865 312263
✉ Email myorders@raintreepublishers.co.uk

Customers from outside the UK please telephone +44 1865 312262

Raintree is an imprint of Capstone Global Library Limited, a company incorporated in
England and Wales having its registered office at 7 Pilgrim Street, London, EC4V 6LB –
Registered company number: 6695582

Text © Stone Arch Books, 2009
First published by Stone Arch Books in 2009
First published in hardback in the United Kingdom in 2009
First published in paperback in the United Kingdom in 2010
The moral rights of the proprietor have been asserted.

Art Director: Heather Kinseth
Graphic Designer: Kay Fraser
Edited in the UK by Laura Knowles
Printed and bound in China by Leo Paper Products Ltd

ISBN 978-1406212563 (hardback)
13 12 11 10 09
10 9 8 7 6 5 4 3 2 1

ISBN 978-1406213584 (paperback)
14 13 12 11

British Library Cataloguing in Publication Data
Lemke, Donald.
The hound of the Baskervilles. – (Graphic revolve)
741.5-dc22

A full catalogue record for this book is available from the British Library.

Northamptonshire
LRE

Askews & Holts

Table of Contents

Introducing (Cast of Characters) 4

Chapter 1
The Great Detective. 8

Chapter 2
Legend of the Hound. 12

Chapter 3
A Dangerous Game 19

Chapter 4
Baskerville Hall 24

Chapter 5
Mystery on the Moor. 32

Chapter 6
The Hound's Next Victim. 42

Chapter 7
Holmes Closes In 48

Chapter 8
Death on the Moor. 58

Introducing . . .

Sherlock Holmes

Sir Henry Baskerville

Beryl Stapleton

Dr John Watson

Jack Stapleton

5

Midnight at Baskerville Hall in Dartmoor, England, Sir Charles Baskerville waits for a visitor.

You're late!

I was getting worried.

Wait, you're not—!

No, it can't be!

THE HOUND!

9

Sir Charles Baskerville of Dartmoor gave the paper to me before his recent death.

It reads, "Herein lies the truth behind the Hound of the Baskervilles . . ."

" . . . A long time ago, the Manor of Baskerville was owned by a man called Hugo."

LEGEND OF THE HOUND

"He was so wicked and cruel that his name was feared throughout the land."

"His evil nature was often ignored and even praised by his comrades."

12

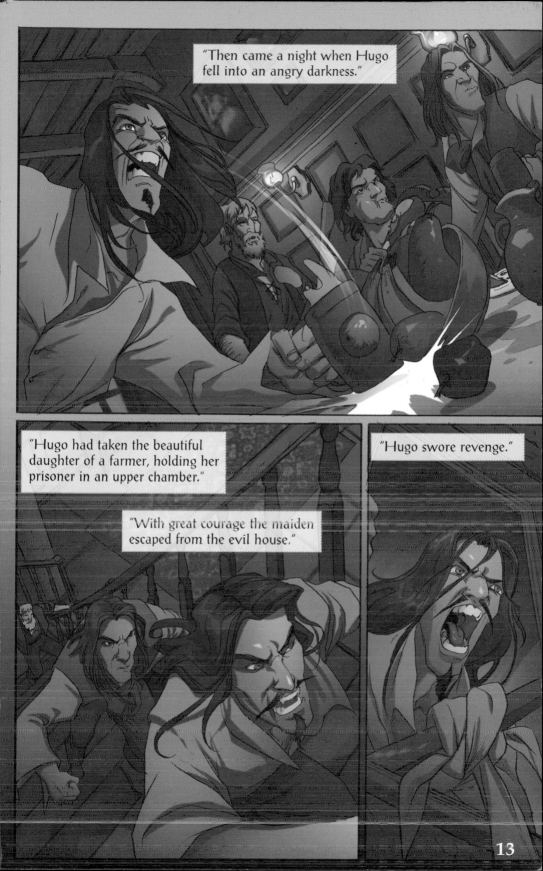

"Then came a night when Hugo fell into an angry darkness."

"Hugo had taken the beautiful daughter of a farmer, holding her prisoner in an upper chamber."

"Hugo swore revenge."

"With great courage the maiden escaped from the evil house."

13

"When Hugo's comrades arrived, they saw something horrible."

"Hugo was also dead!"

"The men swore they saw a great black beast, shaped like a giant hound."

"Such is the tale of the coming of the monster, that haunts the Baskerville family."

Well, Mr Holmes, do you find it interesting?

Only to a collector of fairy tales.

I didn't believe it either.

Then I found footprints where Sir Charles fell the night of his death.

Footprints? Made by a man or a woman?

They were the tracks of a gigantic hound!

The Hound of the Baskervilles!

The next morning . . .

Have you reached any conclusions, Holmes?

People in Dartmoor say they've seen the monster.

But my conclusions, will have to wait

I believe Sir Henry is at the door.

I didn't hear him knock.

Instinct, Watson.

Please come in.

Holmes and I were expecting you.

This is Sir Henry, Dr Watson.

I received a strange message at my hotel this morning. We headed right over.

18

Chapter 3

A DANGEROUS GAME

Moments later . . .

Get your coat, Watson.

That warning was quite fresh. The glue hadn't yet dried!

We must not lose sight of them.

Sir Henry's life may depend upon it!

Just as I thought, Sir Henry is being followed.

The bearded man in that cab is our suspect!

20

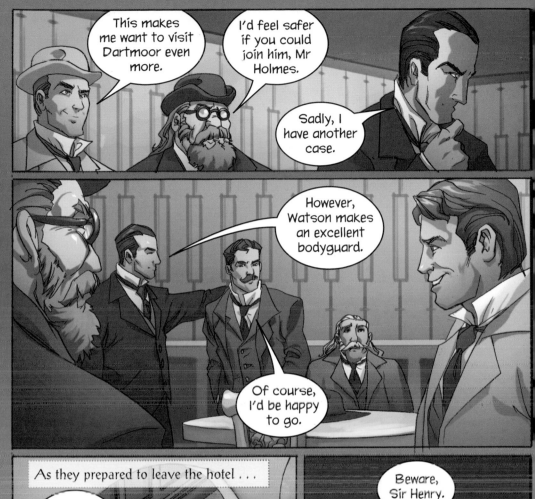

This makes me want to visit Dartmoor even more.

I'd feel safer if you could join him, Mr Holmes.

Sadly, I have another case.

However, Watson makes an excellent bodyguard.

Of course, I'd be happy to go.

As they prepared to leave the hotel . . .

Strange! One of my boots is missing!

Why would anyone steal just one boot?!

Beware, Sir Henry.

This is becoming a dangerous game.

23

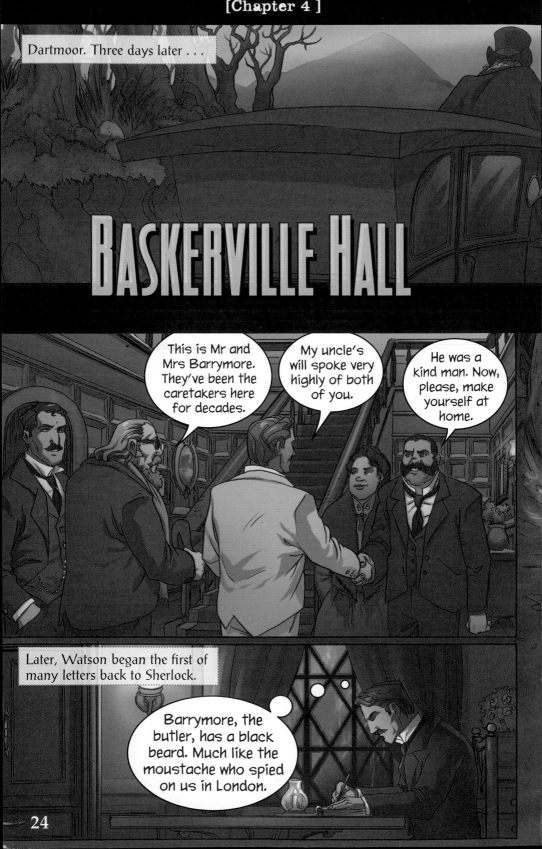

29

MYSTERY ON THE MOOR

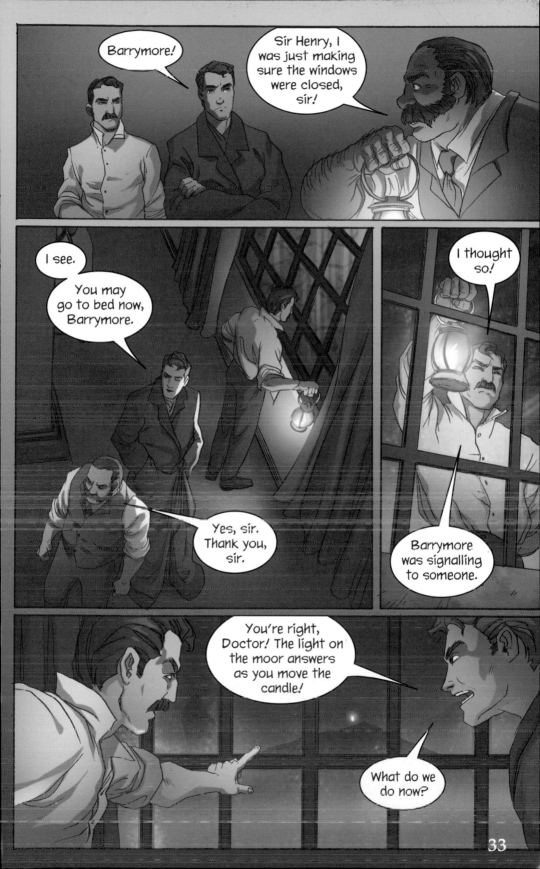

33

"I felt guilty taking Sir Henry with me, but I couldn't leave him alone in that house."

Over there, Doctor!

"I was very glad to have my revolver."

Sir Henry! Look out!!

KRRAASH

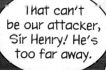

Good morning, Barrymore.

Has Sir Henry already been down for breakfast?

Yes, sir.

He left the house quite early this morning.

Sir Henry on the moor alone? Why would he be so foolish?!

Meanwhile . . .

I shouldn't be here, Henry.

Of course, you should. I love you, Beryl.

37

41

"I left Sir Henry at tea with Dr Mortimer. I continued to think about the puzzle of L.L. as I went to visit Mr Franklin."

THE HOUND'S NEXT VICTIM

Welcome, Dr Watson! This is a great day for me!

I've solved two mysteries of the moor at once!

My, what a beautiful painting!

That's my daughter, Laura.

We haven't spoken since she married an artist named Lyons against my wishes.

Quickly, now! Up to the roof!

What are we doing up here?

I've located the hideout of the madman, Seldon! Look!

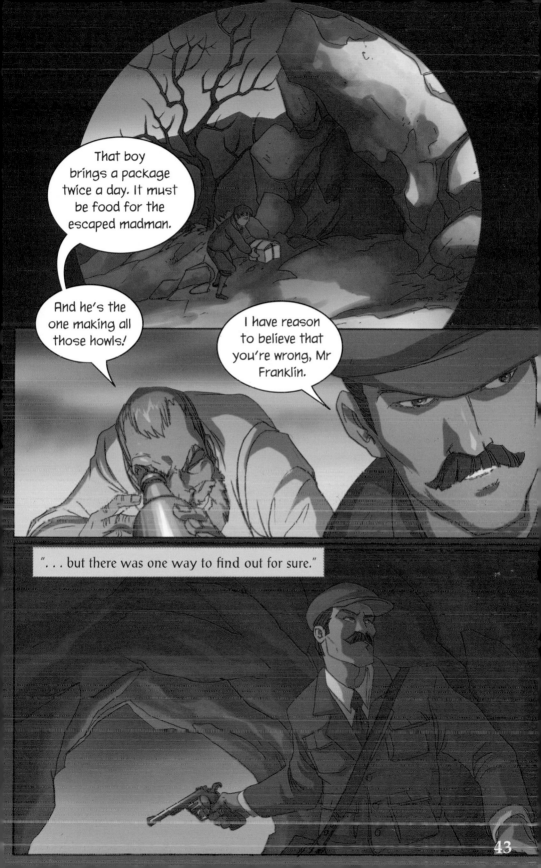

That boy brings a package twice a day. It must be food for the escaped madman.

And he's the one making all those howls!

I have reason to believe that you're wrong, Mr Franklin.

"... but there was one way to find out for sure."

44

47

Chapter 7

Later, at Baskerville Hall . . .

HOLMES CLOSES IN

Mr Holmes, I had no idea you were coming to Dartmoor!

I thought I should.

Are these family portraits, Sir Henry?

Yes, those are the Baskerville ancestors.

He's an unfriendly looking fellow. Do you know his name?

That's Hugo. He started the curse of the Hound!

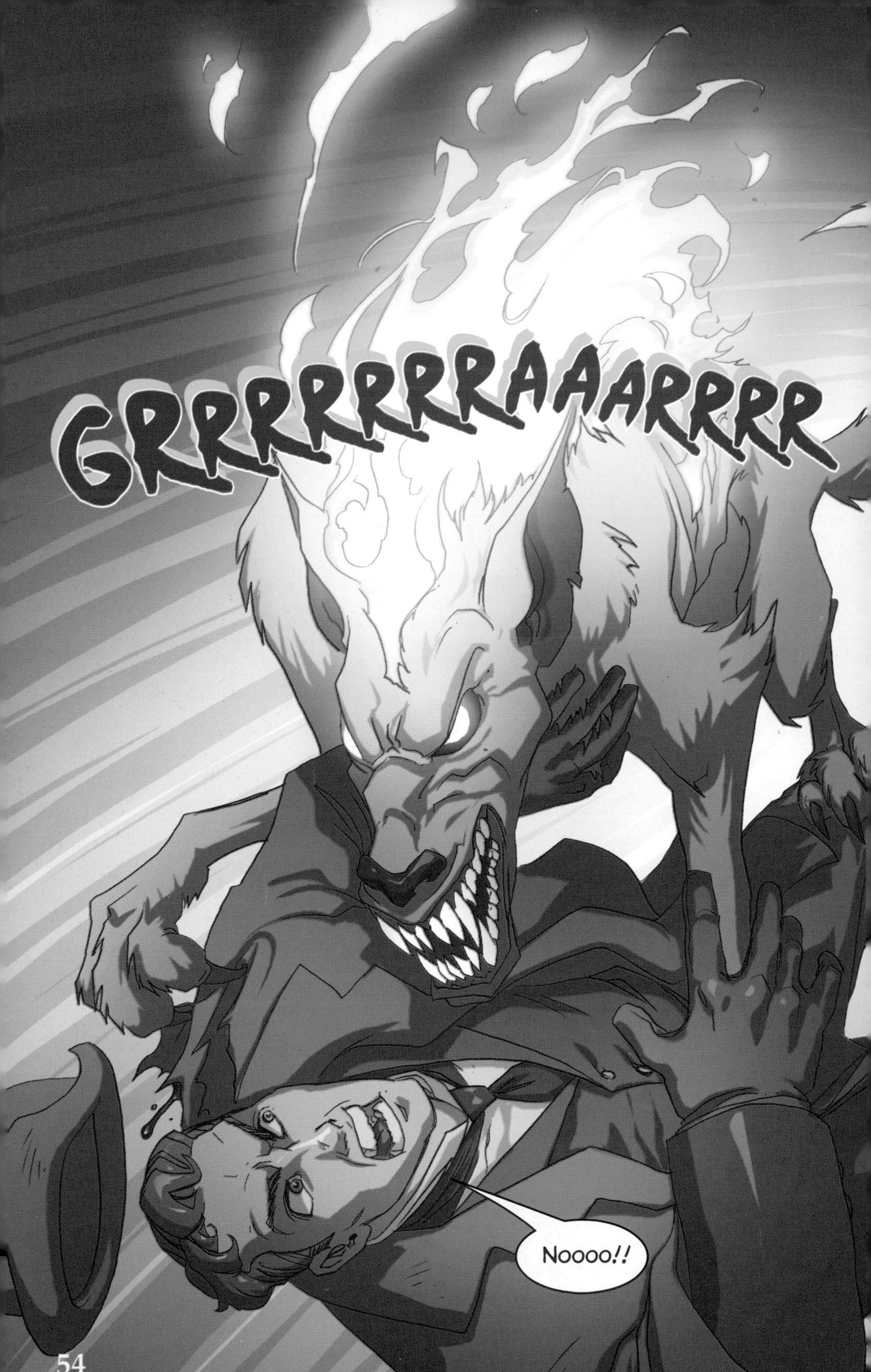
GRRRRRRRAAARRRR
Noooo!!

BLAAM!
BLAM!

BLAAM!

Now, Watson!

It's all right. You're safe now.

What was that thing?

A very large and angry dog.

The animal has been covered with phosphorous paint to make it glow.

Who would do such a thing?

One of the most dangerous men I've ever faced.

Now come, Watson!

55

Moments later at the Stapleton house . . .

KRRAASH

Listen!

There's someone in the cellar.

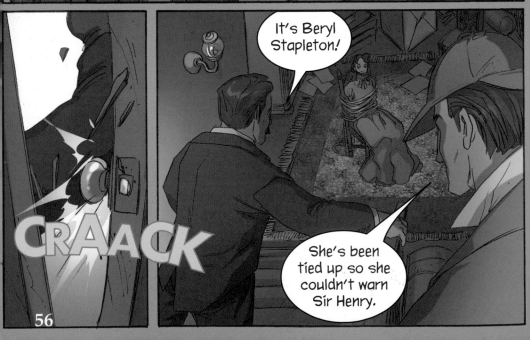

CRAACK

It's Beryl Stapleton!

She's been tied up so she couldn't warn Sir Henry.

Chapter 8

Far out on the moor . . .

DEATH ON THE MOOR

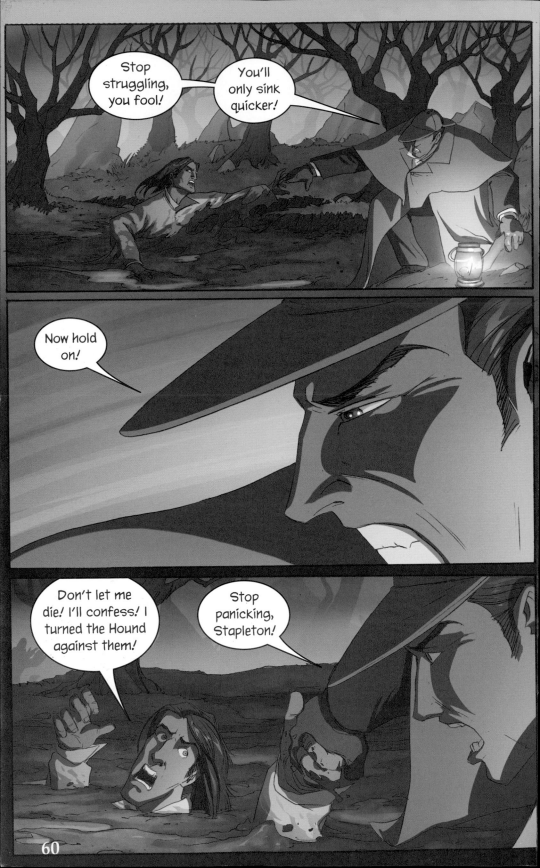

61

Later at Baskerville Hall . . .

My missing boot!

I found it where Stapleton hid the killer hound. He needed something with your scent.

That's why the hound went after Seldon.

He was wearing my old suit!

Exactly.

When your boot was stolen, I knew that we faced a real enemy, not merely a family ghost.

What did Stapleton have against me and my uncle?

Let me show you.

This portrait of Hugo is the very image of Stapleton!

62

Clearly you weren't the only relative in line for the Baskerville fortune, Sir Henry.

Well, I'd say this Stapleton, as he called himself, got what he deserved.

Yes, violence does, in truth, come back upon the violent.

The guilty man always falls into the pit that he has dug for another.

About the Author

Sir Arthur Conan Doyle was born on 22 May, 1859, in Edinburgh, Scotland. In 1885, he graduated with a degree in medicine from Edinburgh University. Shortly after, Conan Doyle opened a successful medical practice in England. While there, he married Louise Hawkins, and the couple soon had two children, Mary Louise and Alleyne Kingsley. Meanwhile, Conan Doyle published several stories including *A Study in Scarlet* in 1887. This was the first story to feature the character Sherlock Holmes. Before his death on 7 July, 1930, Conan Doyle wrote 55 more tales about the world's most famous detective.

About the Retelling Author

Since 1986, Martin Powell has been a freelance writer. He has written hundreds of stories, many of which have been published by Disney, Marvel, Tekno Comix, Moonstone Books, and others. In 1989, Powell received an Eisner Award nomination for his graphic novel *Scarlet in Gaslight*. This award is one of the highest comic book honours.

About the Illustrator

Daniel Perez was born in Monterrey, Mexico, in 1977. For more than a decade, Perez has worked as a colourist and an illustrator for comic book publishers such as Marvel, Image, and Dark Horse. He currently works for Protobunker Studio while also developing his first graphic novel.

Glossary

ancestor (AN-sess-tur) – a relative or family member that lived a long time ago

comrades (KOM-radz) – good friends

convict (KON-vikt) – someone who has been in prison for committing a crime

elderly (EL-dur-lee) – another word for old

fatigue (fuh-TEEG) – great tiredness

identify (eye-DEN-tuh-fye) – to recognize who a person is

loyalty (LOI-uhl-tee) – faithful support of someone

lunatic (LOO-nuh-tik) – a wildly insane or crazy person

maiden (MAYD-uhn) – a young, unmarried woman

mire (MYR) – an area of extremely wet and muddy ground

moor (MOOR) – a grassy area with soft, spongy ground like a bog

phosphorous (FOSS-fur-uhss) – a kind of chemical that glows in the dark

prehistoric (pree-hi-STOR-ik) – happening in a time before history was written down by humans

revenge (ri-VENJ) – an action taken to pay someone back for something mean they did in the past

More About Sherlock Holmes

Sherlock Holmes is the world's most famous detective. In fact, he's so well-known that many people believe he was a real person. However, Sherlock Holmes is actually a fictional character created by author Sir Arthur Conan Doyle.

Although Sherlock Holmes wasn't a true-life detective, his character was based on a real person. While at Edinburgh University, author Conan Doyle studied with a surgeon named Dr Joseph Bell. The author admired Dr Bell's ability to diagnose his patients simply by examining the clues of their illness. Conan Doyle gave Sherlock Holmes the same brilliant detective skills.

So where did the name Sherlock Holmes come from? Some people believe this question remains a mystery. Others, however, think Conan Doyle used the last name of another doctor, Wendell Holmes. The author may have also used the name of violinist Alfred Sherlock.

At age 27, Conan Doyle wrote his first Sherlock Holmes mystery in just three weeks. The story, titled *A Study in Scarlet*, appeared in the *Beeton's Christmas Annual* magazine in 1887. One year later, the story was published as a book with illustrations by the author's father, Charles Altamont Doyle.

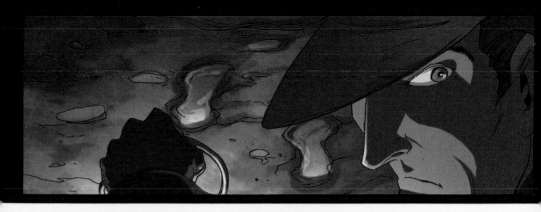

After *A Study in Scarlet*, Conan Doyle wrote a dozen more Sherlock Holmes stories, which appeared in the *Strand Magazine* in London. These stories also included illustrations by artist Sidney Paget. Many people credit Paget for creating the detective's famous look, including his pipe, deerstalker cap, and inverness coat.

By 1893, Conan Doyle decided to stop writing Sherlock Holmes mysteries. In the story *The Final Problem*, the author killed off the great detective. Readers around the world became extremely upset by this decision. At their request, Conan Doyle continued writing Sherlock Holmes mysteries until 1927. Before his death on 7 July, 1930, Conan Doyle had written a total of 56 stories about the detective.

In the stories, Sherlock Holmes lived at 221B Baker Street in London. Today, this real address has been turned into a museum for the great detective. Visitors to the residence can learn more about Conan Doyle, his mysteries, and his character, the brilliant Sherlock Holmes.

1. Do you think Sherlock Holmes could have solved the case without his assistant Dr Watson? How did he help the great detective? Use examples from the story to support your answers.

2. Look back through the story. Who were some of the main suspects in the case? What clues led Sherlock Holmes to the real criminal? Find at least two examples for each question.

3. The legend of the Hound of the Baskervilles turned out to be a hoax. Do you believe in other legendary creatures, such as bigfoot, the Loch Ness monster, and the abominable snowman? Or, do you think these creatures are fake? Explain your answer.

Writing Prompts

1. Sir Arthur Conan Doyle wrote many tales about Sherlock Holmes. Write your own mystery with the famous detective as the main character. What crimes will he solve this time?

2. A legend is a story that is passed down from person to person. Start your own story about a legendary creature like the Hound of the Baskervilles. What will your creature look like? Where does it come from? Then, pass your story on to a friend or family member.

3. Pretend you are the author. Write a new ending to this story where another suspect turns out to be the real criminal.

The War of the Worlds

In the late 19th century, a cylinder crashes down near London. When George investigates, a Martian activates an evil machine and begins destroying everything in its path! George must find a way to survive a War of the Worlds.

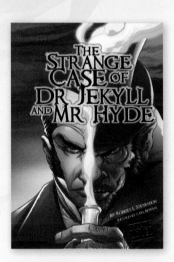

The Strange Case of Dr Jekyll and Mr Hyde

Scientist Dr Henry Jekyll believes every human has two minds: one good and one evil. He develops a potion to separate them from each other. Soon, his evil mind takes over, and Dr Jekyll becomes a hideous fiend known as Mr Hyde.

Gulliver's Travels

Lemuel Gulliver always dreamed of sailing across seas, but he never could have imagined the places his travels would take him. On the island of Lilliput, he is captured by tiny creatures no more than six inches tall. In a country of Blefuscu, he is nearly squashed by an army of giants. His adventures could be the greatest tales ever told, if he survives long enough to tell them.

20,000 Leagues Under the Sea

Scientist Pierre Aronnax and his trusty servant set sail to hunt a sea monster. With help from Ned Land, the world's greatest harpooner, the men soon discover that the creature is really a high-tech submarine. To keep this secret from being revealed, the sub's leader, Captain Nemo, takes the men hostage. Now, each man must decide whether to trust Nemo or try to escape this underwater world.

Graphic Revolve

If you have enjoyed this story, there are many more exciting tales for you to discover in the Graphic Revolve collection...

20,000 Leagues Under the Sea

Black Beauty

Dracula

Frankenstein

Gulliver's Travels

The Hound of the Baskervilles

The Hunchback of Notre Dame

King Arthur and the Knights of the Round Table

Robin Hood

The Strange Case of Dr Jekyll and Mr Hyde

Treasure Island

The War of the Worlds